Bigfoot Sasquatch Files

Volume 9

By Kevin E. Lake

These stories are true.

Potentially...

1

Uncle Burton's Diary

Uncle Burt, as we called him, though I'm sure his mother would have called him Burton, as a child, at times when he was in trouble, was not a rich man. He was a 'just enough to get by and by God grateful for it' kind of guy.

Uncle Burt, like our entire clan, came from hard working stock, where a man's hard work was rewarded by enough to survive, and even better, the affordance of a great night's sleep. Our people never fancied the finer things in life so materialism was never part of our way. I guess it's why I was surprised when I got a call, last spring, telling me that I'd "inherited" something from my recently deceased uncle Burt.

When I found out that my inheritance was merely a diary, a diary I had no clue the man had kept, my mind was set at ease, rather, my mind was set back to reality, as for a fleeting moment I fancied Uncle Burt having had jars of cold hard cash buried around his property, which his attorney had collected and pooled together, and that I had been deemed the lone recipient of all that cold hard cash.

I asked Mr. Esquire, while I had him on the phone, if he could mail the diary. It was then that I was made aware of the very odd condition that came with my inheritance, that being, that I would only accept the diary while in the presence of Mr. Esquire and only in his offices. I would be locked in the drawing room of Mr. Esquire's offices (as his offices were found to be in an old house built in the late 1880's) where I would read the diary, in its entirety, alone, and then burn the diary in the fireplace, which would be burning hot upon my arrival.

As you can imagine, I found this condition quite odd. Why would I, or anyone, drive nearly four hours, in one direction, to read the diary of a recently deceased man who'd, and with all respect given as I say this, never accomplished *anything* that *anyone* would consider meaningful outside of our little village in Appalachiastan?

As I stated earlier, Uncle Burt was one hell of a hard worker. He was an honest man, and boy, could he really spin a yarn. I'd listened to plenty of his yarns in my youth. But the fact of the matter is, the man never made it past the eighth grade, he spent forty years working as a lumberjack, either logging or driving log trucks, and though he'd been all over the mountains of his native Appalachiastan, he'd never left them, save for the time or two when he ventured back to the motherland of Virginia to visit the beach, both times of which he stated upon returning home, he could have "saved time and money heading over to the lake for a dip." He also pointed out that there, "wouldn't have been so damned many other people around, either."

However, just as I was about to decline my inheritance, I remembered something that Uncle Burt had said to me after telling me one whopper of his yarns. He'd told me the story more than forty years ago, and I remember asking him, when he was finished with the telling, if it were true, and he'd told me that as sure as he and I were breathing air, that it was true. When I'd asked him to prove it to me, which he could have easily done at the time, he told me that he feared doing so, because, in his own words, "the thing was so goddamn close to human (and he *never* took the Lord's name in vain), that I'm a'skeered they'll put me away for manslaughter. And I trust you, boy," he'd continued," but not with my life. Look, let me tell you what I've learned about secrets. The only way to keep a secret between three people is if two of them are dead." But even more chilling than this, what he said next led me to believe that the story was true, and I feel as if I've known this for these past forty years. What he said was, "when I'm dead and safe, I'll prove it to you. Beyond the shadow of any doubt, I'll prove it to you."

"Can I come and do the reading this evening?" I asked Mr. Esquire over the phone after having this memory.

"My offices are open until 5:00 p.m., but I can stay a little later if needed," he said.

"If I leave now," I said, "I can be there by five. I'll call ahead if I'm running behind."

"That will do," he said, and we ended the call. Fifteen minutes later, I was on the road, heading back to the hills of Appalachiastan. The whole while driving, I heard uncle Burt's voice in my head. The voice was retelling the stories from all those years ago. But the story that the voice told the most- over and over as if none of the other stories had even mattered- was the story I will relate to you now.

***

Uncle Burt and I had gone native brook trout fishing. For those readers unfamiliar with the activity, I will point out that it's actually a combination of many activities in one. Firstly, it's part hiking. One cannot successfully fish for native brook trout without walking, at least, five or six miles on an average day of doing so. And it's more than the most simple form of hiking, as there's no trail. There is a slippery, rocky creek bank that often winds, with the creek, under laurel bushes, or through rocky ravines hardly surpassible by a billy goat. There are often steep climbs and equally steep descents, often laden with moss covered rocks and logs. There are briar and bramble patches to crawl through, around, or over, and among all these already treacherous obstacles, there lies the occasional rattlesnake or copperhead, both deadly venomous.

Native brook trout fishing requires quite the stalking ability, so it's one part sniper, for lack of a better description. You see, the very small fish, which, technically are not even a form of trout, but rather an arctic char which were left in certain northeastern streams during the last ice age, when the glaciers had actually pushed their way as far south as central West "By God" Virginia, before retreating and melting, are very skittish. Even if a stiff wind blows a tree branch which is hanging above the small pool of water which they inhabit, the small fish will dart under a rock or the edge of the bank and stay hidden, at times, for the rest of the day, upon sight of said tree branch. So, while one is traversing the rugged terrain where the streams are located that house these small fish (catching one of eight inches or more in length is to catch a real monster), one must do so quietly and cautiously. More than once this writer had spent ten minutes or more sneaking up on a beautiful hole of water, maybe three feet wide by the same length, and about a foot deep, only to stumble over a fallen limb or slip on a rock at the last second and sadly see that beautiful six inch long native brook trout dart up underneath the bank on either side, and not come out again for the day.

One must be a naturalist and a keen observer to successfully fish for native brook trout, for you see, there are constantly different types of insects hatching at different times of the year, and in order to have the most success with catches, one must match one's bait to the hatch. If black gnats are hatching like mad the first of June, using what worked only a week before, a may fly pattern dry fly, won't work at all.

And certainly not lastly, one must be quite proficient at casting. It's not just about hitting one's mark on the water, it's about not hitting the many obstacles before the bait even gets there, like numerous tree branches, boulders, logs, bushes, etc.

"Almost there," Uncle Burt said. We had hiked about four miles upstream. We'd set out at first light and it was nearing noon. Four miles of native brook trout fishing on a stream about a foot and a half wide and eight inches deep, on average, with the occasional pools of six feet by six feet that might have been eighteen inches deep, meant that we were making pretty good time. To this day, I hate to admit this, and it certainly isn't the way I would do things if I could go back and do them differently, Uncle Burt and I both had two dozen brook trout each in our plastic bread bags we used to carry our catches in. We put one hell of a hurting on the native brook trout populations in those mountains. And we had a pretty shitty attitude about it, too. You see, we knew that everyone else kept all the fish they caught. "Catch and release" was a practice we viewed as being for the yuppies who came into our areas from the cities to fly fish once or twice a year so they could go back to their doctors and lawyers offices, where they proudly hung their far too expensive Orvis fly rods over their fake, gas burning fireplaces, and prattle on to their patients and clients about how they are prodigious fly fisherman, and of how they brave the natives and travel into the heart of Appalachiastan twice a year, once in the spring and once in the fall, to catch the most elusive fish to be caught in North America. We locals? "Dumb hillbillies," as those yuppies called us in hushed tones?

We, on the other hand, kept and ate every goddamn fish we caught!

"Right up here's the head of it," Uncle Burt said as we made our final push to where this stream actually started. You see, many of these native brook trout streams we fished were so small that they didn't even show up on any of the topographical maps produced by the Forest Service. Many of them simply shot up out of a spring hole at either the top of a mountain or part of the way down one. The streams may run for only a few miles before flowing into a larger stream (these, of course, are called tributaries), but a good many of them simply gave out. One minute, water is flowing, the next, it just stops. Admittedly, very few of the streams that just stopped had any trout in them, but most of the ones that were tributaries did. The one we'd been fishing on that day was a small tributary that flowed into yet another tributary that was actually recorded on a map, but this stream was too small to have been recorded.

Just above us, the whole time we'd been making our way up the stream, there was a road- the type of road called a haul road. It derived its name from the purpose it had been cut through the forest anyway to serve; the hauling logs from mountain to mill.

Uncle Burt had cut the haul road above us the spring before. We were out on a beautiful fall day, and we'd actually pondered weather to go native brook trout fishing on this particular day or turkey hunting. We had chosen fishing over hunting, knowing that winter would soon come to our part of Appalachiastan, freezing the waters of these small streams and burying the land in feet of snow. We could at least hunt in such weather, so we'd chosen to fish while the weather still permitted, though, there was one such time when this writer went fishing on this same stream later in life, at the age of 17, just to prove that fish could be caught in sub freezing temperatures. I caught three on a day when it was 20 degrees fahrenheit. I had to suck on the last eyelet on my fishing rod after reeling in every cast, because the tiny water beads would turn to ice and lock the line so that I could not cast unless unfreezing the whole mess with my mouth first. By catching those three brook trout that day I'd won a bet with a naysayer. Though the naysayer never paid up, I'd proven my point. Despite weather conditions, all animals must eat.

"Let's head up here to the road and have our lunch," Uncle Burt said.

We walked up the hill just below the point where the stream we'd been fishing actually began. Sure enough, it shot up, as a spring, from underneath a huge limestone boulder. I'd noticed while crawling up the bank to get to the haul road, which was already beginning to grow over with new vegetation, that it appeared as if there was a "sister spring" or "twin spring" as they were both frequently called, coming from underneath an entire collection of rocks that looked almost as if they'd been bulldozed over the hill, as if to cover up the stream.

"Looks like another spring," I said to Uncle Burt as I maneuvered over the rocks and reached the road.

"Yeah," he said. But that was all he said. He made his way to what would have been the log landing, the wide point at the end of this haul road, where he would have loaded, with a huge piece of machinery called a log loader, the actual logs he'd cut down and dragged to this collection point onto the back of whatever timber truck he would have driven up this tight, steep, barely surprassible road. FYI, if you have never watched a logging operation, it is worth searching up and watching on YouTube. It is absolutely amazing, some of the places these loggers take vehicles into the woods, and the work they do there. These men, and a few women who work in the industry, manage to take these behemoth pieces of machinery up what are practically trails that would be challenging for a four wheeler, load them up with an entire truck's worth of logs, and then haul them back off of the mountain and to the mills.

"I was up here alone the last day of this job," Uncle Burt said, biting into a Spam sandwich, a hillbilly delicacy. "I'd already hauled all the logs to the landing, here," he said between chews, "and I was just loading them onto the truck. It was a Saturday. I remember that. It's why Billy and Cephus were off. I came out and got the job wrapped up by myself so that on Monday we could start a new job over in the next county."

Uncle Burt described how he was loading the logs onto the truck by way of the log loader, which actually sits on top of the back of the timber truck. Though separate parts, a timber truck is often one large 'do it all' piece of machinery. It's got to be in order to get all the different parts up into the working area conveniently.

"I'd noticed that big pool of water down there," he said, continuing his story. "I'd been glancing over there the whole time I'd swing around to the left there to grab another log to bring over to the right and load up on the truck. I just knew there were trout in there, and if I could just see one, why, I was gonna bring you up here fishing with me."

"I guess you saw one," I said, lifting my bread bag overfilled with fish.

"I reckon you can say that," Uncle Burt said. "Not just one, but two. And they were both about the biggest native brook trout I'd ever seen in my life. Had to be at least a foot long, each."

"My God," I said. At that time, I'd never caught a native brook trout that big. Years later I would catch one that was thirteen inches long, and to this day, nearly forty years later, I've never caught one that big, since.

"*My God* is right," he said. "But what happened next brought me back to my senses real quick."

"What happened?" I asked. I remember being hungry, but I also remember being so into Uncle Burt's story that I couldn't take another bite of my pb & j until he continued.

"Now, you probably ain't gonna believe this next part," he said, and I became even more excited to hear the next part. How could I not? If he'd already told me it was unbelievable.

"Well," he said, continuing, looking down at the ground as if in deep thought, remembering the events of that day, and completely forgetting that he held a delicious, half eaten Spam sandwich in his hand. "While I was still staring down at those two fish, I was swinging the log I'd just picked up in the pinchers around to the right, over toward the truck. And all of a sudden, I hit something. The boom stopped as the log bounced off of whatever I'd hit."

"What'd'ya hit?" I asked.

"Well," he said. "That's just it. I knew the coast was clear. I'd done swung half a dozen other logs through there. There weren't no other people around. We're miles outta town up here. And it couldn't have been an obstruction. Why, I looked down from the cab, and I couldn't see anything. I figured there might have been a kink in the boom gears or something, so I just loaded that log up and kept on going. I loaded eight or ten more logs and filled the whole truck. It was only after that, when I climbed down from the cab that I realized what I'd done."

Uncle Burt hanged his head, not in shame, but in a way that looked remorseful. "What was it?" I asked.

"This here's the part you probably ain't gonna believe," he said. I said nothing, even as a child knowing it was best to give the man the time needed to collect his next spoken words properly.

"I saw," he said, when he finally spoke, "laying right there in the mud, something that looked like the biggest goddamn man I'd ever seen in my life, except it was naked, and covered with hair, and had the face of…"

"Of what?" I asked after he'd trailed off and didn't seem like he was coming back.

"Well," he said. "That's part of the story. See, I guess when I'd swung that big red oak log around, while I was gawkin' over the hill at those fish, this thing, or this guy, just snuck right up on me, and I never saw him, or it, and I smashed him right in the face with that big 'ol log that had to weigh a ton if it weighed an ounce, and I just caved his whole face right in. Looked like the front of his head had been smashed in by a cannonball the size of a large watermelon."

I sat in silence, knowing not what to say. Burt sat in silence, as well, fearing he might say too much. When he finally spoke again, he said, "I'll be goddamned if I didn't go and kill one of them there Bigfoot Sasquatches!"

"No way!" I said.

"Yes way!" he said, and as if he'd never been touched, emotionally, by the retelling of the story, he once again took up eating his delicious Spam sandwich.

"Is this story true?" I asked him. I knew he could tell some whoppers, but the way he'd acted during the telling of this particular story led me to believe that this story was not a whopper, but a confession.

"As sure as you and I are breathing air right now, this story is true," he said.

"Prove it," I said. He told me that he could and that he'd love to, but that the thing he'd killed with the log had so closely resembled a human being that he was afraid that he'd get locked up for manslaughter. He told me he trusted me as much as he trusted anyone, but that one of the cold hard facts that he'd learned about life was that the only way to keep a secret between three people was if two of them were dead. He told me not to worry, though, because he said that when he died, and could no longer be carted off to prison, he'd prove it.

***

For the life of me, I will never cease to be amazed how steep the mountains of Appalachiastan are. No matter how many times I go back, though I'll admit it is not often, and it's intentional, I'm always aghast at the sheer, steep climbs. I spent a couple of years living on the west coast, and folks out there liked to tell me that we didn't even *have* mountains back east. We only had *hills* they claimed. Their Rockies and their Cascades were real mountains, they would tell me. I had to give it to them, because in so many ways they were right. But I'd always challenge these one uppers to come back east with me and hike a day through the Appalachians and see if they could walk the next day. I never got any takers.

I rolled into the offices of Mr. Esquire just as darkness fell. It wasn't quite night yet, it was evening, but being that it was the month of March, and the shifting of the clocks forward had not yet occurred, it was still getting darker a bit earlier than I preferred.

"Are you prepared to follow the instructions as I gave them to you?" Mr. Esquire asked.

"I am," I said. He then handed me the diary, which had a lock on the front of it as well as a sealed envelope. "What's this?" I asked, nodding toward the envelope I held in my left hand, while holding the diary in my right.

"Instructions to find the key," he said.

He grabbed me by the elbow, ever so lightly, and guided me into an adjacent room where a single, straight backed leather chair sat before a raging fire. There was a couch off to the side of the room with an end table beside it. "I'll lock you in from the outside," he said. "When you are finished and want out, simply knock."

"Okay," I said, feeling as if I'd somehow been swept into an early 1900's English novel.

Mr. Esquire left the room. I could hear the lock latch as he turned the key from the outside. I sat in the straight backed chair before the fire and stared into the flames. I found myself thinking that I could not believe I'd just driven four hours to perform such a task. What on earth could be in this diary? And how more could it answer my question from all those years before than by simply stating the story was true? Weren't there better things I could be doing with my time?

Without further thinking or further hesitation I opened the envelope. There was a piece of paper inside, upon which was written a single, simple sentence.

"Look under your cushion."

I stood and pulled up the cushion on the chair upon which I'd been sitting, and sure enough, there was a small, silver key there. I took it up, replaced the cushion, then sat back down before the fire. I put the key in the latch of the diary, opened it, and found that the entire book was empty, save for one page. A page close to the middle had been marked by way of the ribbon marker protruding from the spine of the diary. There was a note here- nay, a letter- and it read…

"K,

If you're reading this, before a blazing fire in Mr. Esquires offices, then I trust you never quite got over your curiosity of the story I told you years ago.

Before I "prove" to you, the truth of my tale, I must first point out my fascination about the single biggest question you never asked me either at the time I told you my tale, or later, when you had nearly forty years to ask it, that question being, 'what did I do with the body?'

I'm glad, K, that you never asked this question, because as an honest man, I was never good at lying, and I feared this question would come from you, and there would be no way I could get out of letting you know the answer. If your lack of questioning in this regard was intentional, I thank you, from my grave, for saving me the awful situation of having to either lie or answer it out right.

With this said, I will now give you the answer to that question you never asked.

I buried it!

Where?

I must first point out that on the day that I told you the story, I did tell one lie. I hesitated, forgetting I held a delicious Spam sandwich in my hand at the time, doing my best to keep a poker face so you would not discover my dishonesty. I suppose it worked.

It wasn't untrue that my mind had been distracted by my viewing of two large native brook trout in the hole of water off to my left. That is very true. The part that is not true is that it was the wrong hole of water.

If you'll remember, as we climbed that creek bank, all those years ago, you pointed out that it appeared as if another stream was coming from another spring which was under rocks- rocks, if you'll remember, that appeared to have been pushed over the hillside by a bulldozer.

K, it appeared as if there was another stream here, coming from another spring, because there was. Before those rocks were there, rocks that I did, indeed, push into the hollow with the blade on the front end of my log skidder, there was a sister hole which appeared nearly identical to the other hole of water that you did see. It was in this hole that two large native brook trout tread water, and into this hole that I did peer, as I carelessly swung a log around to my right, without looking first, and smashing it into the face of a creature that was nearly as human as you and I.

As I mentioned to you the day I told you this story, what I'd killed was so human that I honestly felt as if I might go to prison for killing it. I had not harmed the creature intentionally, and I meant no malice in what I did next, but I was out to save my own hide.

I pushed the creature, which had to have been eight feet tall and weigh nearly eight hundred pounds, over the hill and into that beautiful pull of water where I'd been staring at those beautiful trout, though understandably, trout were the furthest things from my mind by this time. Then, I pushed every large rock and small boulder I could find into the ravine, burying the body with mostly limestone and sandstone, and then I was sure to flatten it out, as best as I could, so as to make it all appear natural. I'll admit that part of taking you fishing there so that you could see the area was to make sure someone who didn't know what had happened wouldn't be able to tell that the land had been manipulated. I guess my workmanship passed the test, at least yours.

Does this prove to you, K, that my story is true? In my mind, it does. In your mind, it might not. If you want further proof from this point, well, that is up to you. You're a clever man. I know you can figure out what to do next if there is a next step for you. As far as I'm concerned, I know I can rest in eternity, having taken this secret to my grave, but also having made my confession posthumous.

Now, burn this diary, you dumb hillbilly!

Love,

Uncle Burt"

***

I sat, staring into the fire, pondering the validity of the "confession" as it were, that I'd just read. Could this be true? Was this a prank from Uncle Burt from beyond the grave? An excellent storyteller he'd always been, but a prankster? It had never been his way.

I stood slowly, tossed the diary into the fire, which was now beginning to burn down a bit, and I sat back down and watched the book burn. After it had burned beyond recognition, I rose, turned and walked to the door. I rapped on it lightly with the knuckle of the middle finger on my right hand. I could hear the more than a century old floor boards on the other side of the room creaking as Mr. Esquire came to free me from my chamber.

As Mr. Esquire opened the door, he held a pillow and a folded blanket. "I know it's quite a drive back to the motherland of Virginia," he said. "And it's getting late. FYI, the couch in the same room in which you are leaving is more comfortable than any motel bed in the county (there *are* no hotels in this part of Appalachiastan- only really shitty run down motels), and if you'd like to spend the night, you're welcome to do so. There is food a'plenty in the kitchen, and you can let yourself out in the morning.

I thought for a minute, and it was obvious that Mr. Esquire could read my thoughts as he grinned at my ponderance. It was not the long drive back to the motherland of Virginia that made me consider staying. It was the certain head of a certain hollow between two certain hills where a stream not located on any topographical maps lay that was piquing my curiosity and tempting me to stay.

"That's kind of you, Mr. Esquire," I said. "I believe I'll take you up on your offer."

He smiled as he handed me the pillow and the blanket. He turned to leave, and as he grabbed the doorknob of the front door, he turned, and simply said, "there are a few things in a sack you might be needing. Just inside the closet, there." With this, he nodded toward a door in the room in which I would sleep before the fire, and then he walked out the front door, shut it and locked it.

With that I was alone.

Out of curiosity, I made my way to the door which he'd nodded toward, opened it, and within found a large, green military style luggage sack. I opened it and found that it contained a pickaxe and a shovel and three pairs of gloves.

I went to the couch, lay out my bedding, got under the blanket and shut my eyes.

But I didn't sleep a wink all night!

***

Around 4:00 a.m. I gave up. What was the use? It was well into the next day, though the sun still lacked a couple hours from rising. I would not wait for it. I would leave. However, my destination was not my comfortable, vast estate back in the motherland of Virginia. It was up one of the deepest, darkest hollows in Appalachiastan. So far up, as our native son and hero Chuck Yaeger would have said, that they "had to pump sunshine into it."

After an hour and a half's drive up several old roads that got only smaller and smaller, more narrow with each passing mile, I came to the point where vehicle would no longer take me, even though said vehicle is a totally awesome Dodge Ram 1500 four wheel drive pick 'em up truck that would make any Prius owner's you know what go limp upon sight. Came now the rest of the journey that could only be made on foot.

I was a mile up the trail when the sun came up bright enough for me to see. I'd had no problem making my way in the pre-dawn light, more like a glow for those late risers who aren't familiar with the light of early dawn, as the old haul road Uncle Burt had cut himself all those years ago still remained, though there were now trees littered throughout it, some nearly two feet in diameter. Time marches on, saplings and seedlings become mighty trees, and men and women grow old.

An hour after the sun had risen, I reached my destination. The old log landing on top of the mountain. Though I remain, to this day, in great shape, participating in the occasional 5k road race for charity, it had been so long since I'd hiked up one of those "hills" in Appalachiastan, and I was reminded of the challenge I used to give my mates back on the west coast- the challenge that none of them ever accepted- and it damned near got the best of me.

Without wasting any time I began removing rocks that made flat land of where I knew originally there was a ravine. Though temperatures had been in the eighties the day before when I'd left my beautiful home in Virginia, the temperatures, at this high elevation in Appalachiastan, hovered around forty. There was still snow and ice, and it made for a slower go of it, but rock by rock, stone by stone, I made my way through the earth. After an hour's time of work, I reached running water. The original spring.

But I found nothing.

No skeleton, no skull, no nothing.

"I'd been had!" I said to myself, sitting beside the bank well into mid morning. I opened the old military luggage sack again and took out two sandwiches I'd made just before leaving the offices of Mr. Esquire. Havarti cheese and uncured salami on wheat bread with fat free mayonnaise. Mr. Esquire and I, it appeared, had similar tastes in cheese and meats. I could not imagine how far Mr. Esquire had driven, though, to find the havarti, for they certainly did not sell havarti cheese in the part of Appalachiastan where his offices were located.

"That's it!" I said, thinking of Mr. Esquire. "They are in on it together!"

And they had to be. How could they not be? The way Mr. Esquire had simply told me of the tools in the sack in the closet. Tools he knew would come in handy for some sort of digging. How could he not have been aware of that for which I'd be digging?

Further, he'd intentionally lured me into staying the night at his offices. He seemed far too ready with that pillow and blanket when he'd unlocked the door and opened it. It was as if he wanted to make sure I did not flee.

"Those sons-a-bitches!" I said, peeling the crust off my sandwich and throwing it to the other side of the water hole that I'd uncovered. It was then, and only then, that my thoughts stopped in their tracks.

The bit of bread I'd tossed to the other side of the water hold had been caught, just above ground level, by what appeared to be a stick. But this stick was not quite the color of any stick I'd seen before. At most, it resembled the color of a sycamore tree, but there were no sycamores in the area. Further, the end of it appeared to have been whittled, by a knife, and the odds of such a thing seemed completely remote to me.

I stood, and already wet from the knees down, walked through the water and to the other side of the small pool. I bent over to inspect the bread and the "stick" upon which it had been caught. This is when a sudden terror came over me, as I realized this was no stick.

It was a bone.

A finger bone!

But unlike any finger bone I'd ever seen (not that I'd seen many finger bones, if any), it was huge!

I removed the bread crust from the bone and then began removing some of the other stones and soil around the finger. What I found was that this finger was attached to an entire hand!

I've attended only one NBA basketball game in my life. It was the Washington Wizards vs. the Miami Heat, and the game had been held in Washington, D.C. This was during the second, and what would be the final year of Michael Jordan playing for the Wizards, as well as in the NBA, despite having already retired twice before this. I knew that seeing Jordan play (Shaquile O'neal was playing that night, as well, for the Heat), live, would be a piece of history that I would regret missing if I didn't go to at least one game that year, and to this day, I'm glad I did.

My point here is that during that game, I remember being so impressed by how small the basketball looked in the hands of those NBA players. They palmed the basketball like I would palm a baseball. Their hands were that big! And I explain this to the reader, now, because what I can tell you of the skeletal remains of the hand I unearthed that day in the spring which had formerly been hidden for the past forty years would have made those NBA players' hands appear as small as their hands made my hand appear to be.

"Oh, my God!" I said, as I stared at the hand, now coming up from the soil and the rocks. And it was so much more than just a hand. It was a hand that was attached to a wrist, which I would assume was attached to an arm, which was attached to a torso, etc. etc. "Oh, my mother fucking God!"

Immediately, without taking the time to think, I climbed out of the ravine, bringing my luggage sack and tools with me. Tired as I was, I made sure to bury the hand and the pool itself with a couple feet's worth of stone and rock. I hadn't covered it nearly as well as Uncle Burt had forty years before, but I'd covered it enough to allow that which had been hidden for an equal period of time to remain hidden going forward.

Fortunately, the long walk back to my totally awesome, like new Dodge Ram 1500 4x4 pick 'em up truck that would make the you know what of any Prius owner go limp upon sight was all downhill. Once back to my truck, I threw my supplies in the back seat and began the long drive back to my beautiful, comfortable, vast estate in the motherland of Virginia. I did not return Mr. Esquire's sack and the tools within, but I will be sending them back UPS (because the post office sucks!).

And I am certain that Uncle Burton's secret, the secret that he took to the grave, will become a secret once again, once either Mr. Esquire or myself pass on to the other side.

The End

2

Are They Hunters? Or Haint They?

"This one would be easy to solve," comment number 87 said. "Just go talk to the neighbors and see if they're letting people hunt on their land."

Of course every other word of the sentence you just read was misspelled before I fixed it.

"I'm done!" read comment number 103. "This asshat could easily go up there and talk to the people on the next property and find out if they hunt or if they let other people hunt on their land. This guy is so fake. He is a scam artist. If you really want to see Bigfoot, come over to my channel (name of channel omitted), where I will show you real proof."

Ah, the joys of working in social media, where everyone's an expert, a critic, and just an all around asshole in general.

Okay, not those of you reading this book. Especially if you read all of the preceding volumes before it. Honestly, you guys are part of the select few that keep me going. I know that not everyone who watches the videos on my YouTube channel "Homesteading off the Grid" is a vertically challenged individual who lives under a bridge.

There's just so damn many of them!

Okay, what is this tirade about?

It's about a series of just a few videos that I uploaded between Christmas of 2020 and just after the New Year of 2021. In the videos, we could very clearly see at least one, at times two, and potentially three upright walking, bipedal creatures. In all of the videos, it was just before dark, and they were spotted toward the top of the hill behind my property, close to where the property line is with one of my neighbors. In one of the videos, the culprits were clearly caught walking toward the setting sun in the west, and in another, they were captured walking away from the setting sun, heading east. In one of the videos, it appeared as if what may have been the third of these "entities" (I'll refrain from calling them 'creatures' at this time, as the jury is still out), actually shimmied up a tree and then simply vanished.

There's a bit of backstory to these videos, and I believe it's worth noting here, though I did note most of it in the videos themselves, but it bears repeating.

There are three things I love most in this life. My wife, our son, and my afternoon naps. I have a real love hate relationship with my afternoon naps in the winter because of the short daylight hours. It's actually easier for me to grab my naps in the winter, because the weather outside is often such that I can easily choose not to do any work outside on bad days without feeling guilty, and I can choose, instead, to nap in front of the woodstove- if aforementioned wife and son are not home- or I can nap upstairs in the bed that's in my office- the very room in which I sit now as I write these words. It helps that there is no gardening or lawn work going on in the winter. Winter is the time of year in which I get most of my reading, writing, well, and napping done.

Oh, and another part of these naps? I wear earplugs. My wife and our son have not learned the fine art of verbally communicating with each other by actually walking into the same room where the other is before addressing them. So, if I want to actually get to sleep and stay to sleep if my family is home, I have to use earplugs. They help, unless my son lets our psychotic cat, Cleopatra, in or out of the house, as my son, who is now ten as of this writing, has not mastered the fine art of shutting a door without slamming it.

I digress.

But that's what I do.

And supposedly (ooh, the word 'potentially' was almost appropriate here, but not quite), you folks who have made it to volume nine of this epic endeavor that has no planned end in sight like that.

So, anyway, I remember the first time I saw the figures on the hill above my house. I'd been taking one of my beautiful, beautiful naps, and when I awakened, I glanced out my bedroom window that faces the back of our property. I stared up into the beautiful, beautiful woods, as I so often do, trying to gauge how much daylight I might have left to go outside and split and stack some firewood, not just a necessary chore due to our lifestyle, but one of my most enjoyable hobbies. I honestly believe I would cut, split and stack firewood even if I didn't have a woodstove or a fireplace, I love doing it so much.

There have been times I've laid in bed, watching out the window, that I've seen deer walking through the woods or in my field or meadow. I've seen hawks, turkeys and even bears. But on this particular late afternoon in December of 2020, I saw something out my window that had me bolting straight up and my heart racing.

Two of them!

I'd seen what appeared to be, at first, two men walking through the woods. Actually, 'walking' isn't the best description here. A better term might be 'stalking.' For you see, it was as if each of the two figures had been hiding behind a tree- separate trees- and almost like synchronized swimmers, they moved from behind the trees hiding them, and simply positioned themselves behind trees that were only a few feet behind the original trees, again, both choosing to hide behind separate trees.

Now, I'll point out that my mind had already decided that I would not be going out and splitting and stacking any firewood, because there couldn't have been twenty minutes of daylight left. This was late December, when the days are shortest, when it gets dark at 5:00 p.m. It was a quarter till five, so the best I could do, as I saw it at the time, was to remain in bed, still as a church mouse, and keep my eyes on the trees where the two figures seemed to be hiding. I watched, until it was too dark to see outside, and I did not see the figures come back out from behind those trees.

I hadn't had my smartphone with me that first day that I saw the figures in the woods from my window, but I made sure to take it upstairs with me when I napped every day after that. Sure enough, three days later, my mysterious figures returned. It was as if they'd been watching me nap the whole while, from a distance of nearly a quarter of a mile away, and then began heading up the hill once they'd noticed I'd woken up.

This time, having my smartphone, I was ready for them. I actually opened my window and walked out onto the snow and ice covered roof to record them. Probably not the smartest idea I'd ever had, but I wanted to get the scene on camera. I did, though I could not detect the perpetrators in the video, so I took things a step farther and uploaded and published the video to my YouTube channel, hoping maybe some of our viewers could spot the beings. No one did, to my knowledge, and I'm sure the whole thing made me look like a paranoid, delusional schizophrenic. But hey, when the word "crazy" is part of your nickname, you don't allow such trifles to bother you and you live the way you want to live, despite what others who see you doing so care or say. We've all heard the saying, "dance like nobody's watching." I've tweaked that a bit to my liking, which is "I dance like I don't give a fuck who's watching," and there is a difference, and I'm willing to bet that if you're reading this book, meaning you've made it this far with me on this journey called life, you totally get the difference. Peas in a pod we are, you salty old soul!

Anyway, as much as I really hated to do it, I put off my naps for the next several days. I wanted to make sure that I was awake, and outside, and armed and loaded with my smartphone when and if these sons-a-gunses came back.

And they did come back!

On two separate occasions!

Long story short (I know, too late), I captured the figures on camera and published the capture in two separate videos. You can go to my YouTube channel "Homesteading Off The Grid" and watch the videos and clearly see these figures for yourself. The titles of the videos are, "VINDICATED!!! He Clearly Captures TWO Of Them Walking Through The Woods On Camera! TWICE!!!" and "Two Stand Guard At The Top Of The Hill While A Third Swings THROUGH THE TREETOPS To Take The Candy!" The titles are long and so are the videos, but hey, that's me, and you can see 'em.

Though I could not tell, from the distance, exactly what the figures were- neighbors, hunters, trespassers, or... wait for it...

Bigfoot Sasquatch!

...I was tickled pink to get it on video and upload and publish it to the channel. For years now, since I've been pursuing what in the hell ever it is that may or may not live in the woods behind my home, I have been called crazy, paranoid, a drug addict, and many, many other things. Like the title of the first of the two videos suggests, I was happy to finally be vindicated.

Or so I thought.

Though I've worked in social media for more than ten years now, and though I understand it to be the gutter of the internet better than anyone, my best- actually capturing these unexplainable entities on camera- still wasn't good enough, as evidence by the way this story started, as well as the hundreds of other similarly flavored comments left on those videos.

So, you might be asking, what's the big deal about going up and asking your neighbors if they hunt or if they allow others to hunt on their property?

Okay, here's the big deal.

It's none of my goddamn business what my neighbors are doing or allowing others to do on their properties!

Nor is it any of my neighbor's goddamn business what I do, or what I allow others to do on my property.

It's as simple as that.

Well, you might ask, why not explain the situation to your neighbor, and yada yada yada...

Because it doesn't matter!

Many people who watch our videos have no idea what it's like to live out in the country and in the south. Sure, there's that stereotypical southern charm shit we're known for, and a lot of it's real, but when it comes to a man's (or woman's) home here in the south, which includes their laid, that is his or her castle, and one really needs to view that property line as a mental moat, because if crossed, uninvited, one faces meeting real life crocodiles in the form of the land or homeowner meeting you with a firearm, and the fact that your property borders there's doesn't make a lick of a shit's difference. If you go uninvited and unwanted (and trust me, if you've not been invited, it's because you're not wanted), you stand to face a good ass-whooping, to have no-trespass papers served against you, or getting shot!

And yes, I'm serious!

"My neighbors in my subdivision aren't like that, thank God," people have commented on videos where I've pointed this out.

I've held back responding to these people thus: "Dear yuppie. That's why you live in a subdivision, and we country folk don't. Please do us all a favor and stay in your subdivision (we actually had a couple yuppies from a subdivision buy a property close by and what asshole nightmares *they* were for a couple years- always wanting to come over and 'pull on your ear' if they saw you out- faking an interest in *how* you're doing to find out *what* you're doing- fucking assholes). Oh, and keep driving your Priuses, because we need all the gasoline for our big four wheel drive pickups and SUVs."

Sorry, I regress.

But that's what I do.

Most call it a segway in storytelling.

And FYI, I've had dealings with these bastards that live around me. Most notably, the annoying neighbor I drove off with the crayon. But that's not the property in question here. This guy, and I've had one dealing with him as well, and it was pleasant and cordial, would eat that guy for lunch. Once, our first year here, when a large tree limb from a large oak had fallen right on our property line, I made my way back to his multi-million dollar spread and asked permission to cut it up. I told him I wasn't sure exactly where the line was, so I wanted to ask permission first. He thanked me for asking, told me to take it, as well as any other free fallen timber or branches or sticks that are close to the line and to never, under any circumstances step foot on his property again. He didn't care about me, my family, what we did, where we've been. He assured us that he felt we were pretty good people, just by the way we asked before taking that limb, but he wanted us to understand fully that he didn't give a goddamn about us or anyone else, thank you, have a good day.

My take on it?

He is the perfect neighbor in my book, because I feel the very same way about him and the rest of the people who live around me. I have always viewed friends, neighbors, and business associates as three separate entities that should never mix, and for the life of me, I can't understand why so many other people cannot grasp that simple concept.

Oh well, for them there are subdivisions.

So, I'm no expert on getting on well with neighbors, but I know a guy...

Okay, that was my lame impression of that Pawn Stars guy that inspired all those memes years ago. But I actually do know a guy who lives on the foot of the mountain behind my house, at the other side of the guy's property I just described. It's not so much a mountain as it is a hill in a series of mountains; the Blue Ridge Mountains to be specific.

We're going to call this guy Carl, because that's not his real name. If one were to walk up the hill behind my house, to the point where we captured the two, if not three figures on film, you would hit the top of the hill which consists of about one thousand acres, which is now split up and owned by half a dozen different families. It was once all part of one piece of property, but the guy who bought it last in its entirety has sold it off piecemeal over the years. The original house he'd built up there was worth about a million, but I guess the woman who bought it from him considered it substandard living, so she immediately put another million dollars worth of upgrades in it.

Once you cross down the other side of the hill, you hit Carl's land. Carl probably has half a dozen acres or so, like myself. Carl is about seventy years old and retired (I'll not say from what), and he strikes me as a gentleman homesteader, much like myself. However, he actually has some horses and cows and chickens, whereas I just have some chickens and rabbits, and potentially, a few head of Bigfoot Sasquatch.

Now, to be honest about it, I rode my mountain bike up the road that goes up that hill behind my house once. I was scared half to death the whole time I was doing it, because of reasons I've mentioned earlier. Some folks wouldn't hesitate a bit to blow a mountain biker off of his mountain bike with a shotgun. The road itself is a state road, which legally means one can travel on the road, but let me tell you, there is court house laws, and then there are country laws, and some folks wouldn't hesitate to drag your mountain bike just inside their property line once they blasted you off of it with their twelve gauge.

I can hear you as you're reading this. "I don't think these people, especially if they're so rich, would behave this way, Crazy Lake."

What I would say to you is, "you don't know too many rich Rednecks."

As it happened, I was out jogging past Carl's homestead around mid-January, about a week after I'd captured whatever I'd captured on video, and I saw that Carl was out. Now, I'd waved at Carl a time or two, and he always waved back, but he never smiled. In "out in the country" body language that means, "I'll be friendly to you and wave at you in passing, but for the love of Christ don't waste my time trying to come over here and talk to me."

I took a big chance that day, because I'd actually intended to jog up the mountain. Since I'd been up there once on my bike and hadn't been shot, I was willing to take the chance. I knew the mountain was steep, but I wanted to see if I could get a glimpse of anything strange from a closer vantage point.

"Excuse me, Sir," I said, slowing down as I got closer to Carl. He was petting one of his horses which was on their side of the fence, just off from the side of the road. "Is it okay if I jog up that road? Or do you think I'll get shot?"

"Well," he said, taking the hand he'd been scratching his horse behind the ear with and beginning to scratch behind his own ear. "I don't want to say you'd get shot, but there's some assholes live up there that would probably come out and tell you what for if they saw you."

"Oh," I said, deflated.

"It's a state road," he continued. "But you know how assholes are."

"I do," I said. "I found out real quick shortly after I moved in." I went on to tell him, the brief version- not the eighteen minutes and thirty six seconds long version- of my experience with the annoying neighbor I had to run off with a crayon.

"If he ever comes back," he said, referencing the annoying neighbor. "Just pick up the biggest stick you can find and go upside his head with it."

"Really?" I said.

"Yeah," he said. "Oh, (name omitted, but he was talking about the annoying neighbor) ain't nothing but an old pervert. He got fired from the university for being a peeping Tom."

"Really," I said.

"Yeah," he said again. "Really."

I got some more dirt on the old pervert hay collector, dirt that so far has turned out at least four more totally awesome short stories (remember a few volumes back? When our heroine Jane took 'ol PT back to Appalachiastan and had him disappeared? Well, that's where that story came from- but how did I write it before Carl told me about it? Well, some of this is being told out of order- I mean, I *am* a storyteller- but you get the point), and then I got to the point.

"I'm curious," I said to Carl. "And it's none of my business, but I'm just curious. But do you know if any of them assholes up there have been hunting or allowing others to hunt on their property above mine lately?" I didn't have to tell Carl where I lived, because that's another thing about country life. I'd been here four years by this time, so I guarantee you everyone with five miles of me knows where I live. And, since I jog and mountainbike all over the place, I can pretty much tell you who lives where within a four or five mile radius of my house.

"Been hearing gunshots?" Carl asked, and I could tell by the way he cocked one eye when he looked at me, and by the tone of his voice when he asked, that he knew I'd not been hearing any gunshots.

"No," I said.

"Then why would you think that there may be someone hunting up there?"

"Well," I began, and then I gave him the short version of the story I've written of here, in regard to the two videos I recorded and published on YouTube. After I finished my story, Carl just stared at me, saying nothing.

"Well," I said. "Are they hunters or ain't they?"

"What you should say," he said, "is, are they hunters or haint they?"

"That's what I said," I said.

"No," Carl said. "You said ain't. I said haint."

"Haint," I said. "You mean like ghosts?"

"Well, you're a southern boy, afterall, aren't ya," Carl said, and he lightened up and laughed for the first time.

"Not really," I said. "I grew up across the state line in Appalachiastan, but I've spent the majority of my adult life over here."

"I thought you talked funny," he said, and then he laughed again. "Hey, did you know the toothbrush was invented in Appalachiastan?" He asked.

"Yeah, I know," I said, rolling my eyes, "because if it had been invented in any other state it would have been called the teethbrush."

"I bet you've heard 'em all, haven't you," Carl said, his laughter finally dying down.

"Yeah," I said.

"Okay," Carl said, serious now. "All I'll tell you, is that there's been times, all around these parts, when folks have thought they've seen people out hunting or trespassing in general on their land. They've run out, sometimes guns a blazin', to run 'em off, only to get almost right up on 'em and have 'em disappear, as if into thin air."

"Really," I said.

"Boy, you love that word, don't you," Carl said, and then he kept on talking like I'd never spoken at all.

"And there's been some folks," he continued, "who have sworn the folks they'd run up on were wearing civil war uniforms. Some blue. Some gray."

He paused and looked at the ground, as if in deep thought. I remained silent, not wanting to interrupt his train of thought, but after he went past the standard eleven seconds of silence no American can comfortably take any longer while in conversation I spoke again.

"Do you believe them?"

"Believe, 'em," he said, and he laughed again. "I not just believe. I agree with 'em, because I've experienced it myself."

"Really?" I said.

"Back to that word again," he said, chuckling. "Oh, every few years or so, I see 'em. I call 'em the sentries. Like you, I've noticed 'em up on the top of the hill, up on that asshole's land there. So I never went up and approached 'em. But I used to be friends with that old asshole up there, back when he owned the whole mountain, before he drank away most of his money he'd inherited and became paranoid about everyone and everything. What I'll tell you is he don't hunt and he don't allow no one else to hunt up there, either. And you aint' seein' no trespassers."

"So you're telling me I'm seeing ghosts," I said.

"You say last week was the first time you've seen 'em?" he said.

"Yeah."

"And you've been out here for four years now?"

"Yeah."

"Sounds about right," he said.

"What do you mean?" I asked.

"That's about how long it's been since I've seen 'em," Carl said. "And they stay pretty regular. Every few years, no more than five years apart at most, they come around. Doin' their rounds."

I couldn't believe what I was hearing, but I fully did believe what I was hearing.

"I'm gettin' up there in years," Carl said. "And my vision isn't quite what it used to be. Nor is my memory. I used to remember to look up there and see if I could see 'em, but I guess I'd forgot almost plum about 'em until you just brought it all back up."

"Wow," I said. "That is freaking amazing."

"Guess they don't believe in that stuff where you come from," he said, as if he felt I was doubting his story.

"Oh, no," I said. "Quite the opposite. Especially with me, personally." I hesitated a minute, but figured I'd strike while the iron was hot. "Have you ever seen or heard tell of any cryptids out here?"

"Any what?" Carl said, obviously having never heard the word before.

"Cryptids," I said. "You know, like Bigfoot Sasquatch."

Carl looked me straight in the eyes, with a look on his face that was as serious as a heart attack, and said, "why you wise ass little punk."

"What?" I said.

"So I tell you I've seen some civil war ghosts, and you're gonna go and call me crazy like that?"

"Crazy!" I said. "I wasn't trying to call you crazy. I was trying to find out if there's been any Bigfoot Sasquatch sightings around here, because frankly, when I saw those figures, I thought that might be what it was."

"Bigfoot," he said, disapprovingly. "Sasquatch."

"Yeah," I said, and I stood, speechless, as did he. We were having a stare down and a saying nothing down. He who spoke first would surely lose.

"Bigfoot Sasquatch," he said.

"Yeah," I said. Again we stood at a stalemate.

Suddenly, Carl threw his head back with the most maniacal laughter I'd heard in years. "Bigfoot Sasquatch! Hole-e-hell-shit boy! Ah hahahaha. Bigfoot Sasquatch!" And he continued to laugh.

"That's okay, Carl," I said and I turned to leave. "You don't have to call me crazy, either."

I began jogging back toward my house, on the other side of the asshole's mountain above us, and I heard Carl shout out, "hey" after I'd gotten about twenty yards away from him.

I stopped, and I turned to look at Carl. He was standing by his horse, giving me a look as serious as he'd given me any other time that day. "Around here," he said, "we just call him

Sasquatch," and then he turned and began walking up the hill toward his house.

I ran back to where we'd been standing while we'd been talking and shouted at Carl as he walked away. "So you've seen him, too?" I asked. "Have others?"

Carl simply threw his hand up in the air, to both wave at me and to wave me off. He never spoke again, and he never turned back around to face me. Discouraged, I turned and was back on my way to finish my run.

I've seen Carl a couple of times since that day, and each time I've started to either jog toward him or bike toward him to follow up with the questions he wouldn't answer that day, and both times, he saw me coming, and he conveniently darted back to his house.

I guess, in a way, that's Carl's way of giving me the answer I was looking for, anyway.

The End

3

The Unfortunate Demise Of Dirty Dick

(Originally Titled: The Unfortunate Demise Of The Dirty Dick)

"We have a problem," sheriff's deputy Burt Reynolds said to Dr. (honorary) Drake as he took off his patrol cap and held it in front of his crotch, as if trying to hide a woody. Drake, who'd been at the side of his house splitting firewood, the old fashioned way, with a ten pound sledge hammer and a diamond maul, had seen him pull up the long drive and walked over at the end of the drive to meet him.

"What's the problem, Bandit?" Drake asked, holding in a laugh.

"Yeah," Reynolds said, emotionless, "like I said when we first met, that one never gets old." He glanced over Drake's shoulder at the work he'd been doing. He mentally noted that Drake appeared to have literal dump truck loads of logs on his property, most of which, it appeared, had already been split into firewood and stacked neatly to season. "You cutting and splitting all this by hand?" he said.

"Yeah," Drake said.

"You need a gas powered log splitter."

"People who can't, or who don't, being critical of people who can, or who do, never gets old," Drake said.

"Touche," Reynolds said. "Look," he spoke again, quickly. "We got something we've got to deal with."

"What asshole who I'm sure deserved it went missing this time?" Drake asked, resting his ten pound sledge hammer at his right side and resting most of his body weight on that.

"No one," Reynolds said. "Well," he hesitated. "There was a postal worker just before Christmas past, but..."

"But?" Drake said.

"I was in there to mail something out once. Just as she was going on her lunch break. Trust me, that bitch deserved it, so I never came to see you."

Drake said nothing. He continued to look at Reynolds, waiting for the reasoning of his business that constituted his visit. Most people, at surface value, would think that one of Drake's greatest combined blessings and curses was his astute ability to locate, communicate with and live in peace and harmony with the various cryptids around the world. An ability that had garnered him both internet fame and a huge following of vertically challenged individuals who lived under bridges who absolutely hated his guts. But if one were to ask Drake himself what he felt his biggest combination blessings with a curse was, he would tell them that it was his amazing people skills that made him come across as so approachable and folksy. He had an aura that made people feel as if he'd never met a stranger. So many people felt like they could just sit and have coffee with him and solve the world's problem from his front porch. The problematic curse of this, which Drake would point out? He didn't hate people, but he had no use for them in general, and he viewed spending any time with them, outside of his family and the less than a handful of very carefully chosen confidants, and extreme waste of his time, which he guarded closely and greedily, and he preferred the masses would simply leave him the ever loving fuck alone.

"Why are you here," Drake finally said, the point of the previous paragraph made.

"There's a girl sitting down at the station right now. A college girl from down at the university. She's getting grilled by this asshole out of D.C.- Manassas, really- for something I know she didn't do. And he's trying to link her to a whole shit ton of shit she didn't do."

"Like what?" Drake asked.

"All these assholes around here who deserved to disappear did that," Reynolds said.

"Oh," Drake said. "You mean like Jittery Jay, Whorrie Torrie, Crazy A and the like?"

"Yeah," Reynolds said. "There was one in particular that put her on this guy's radar. Some old sick fucker that used to work on the grounds crew over at the university. Went by the name "P.T.," both because those were his initials and also because he was a peeping tom. I guess he'd actually been fired for it once, but the union got him his job back. Someone claimed this girl, Jane, her name is, was seen hanging out with the old fuck just before he, well, had an unfortunate demise of sorts and was never seen or heard from again. So this dick from Manassas- who, by the way, is a detective and who is named Dick- is trying to connect this poor girl to all the other unexplained deaths."

"I thought you attributed all those to bear attacks," Drake said. "How could he even draw a link between those passive aggressive, gaslighting lunatics Jittery Jay and Crazy A and someone like that old whore Torrie who'd obviously been mauled to death by a wild beast and some college girl?"

"I know it doesn't make any sense," Reynolds said, "but I sure could use your help on this one. This old bastard's got his hooks in this young girl, and I need to get him off of her."

"I bet she's really torn up," Drake said, looking down, pondering in his mind how he might be able to help. How could he convince some FBI dick, named Dick, that whoever this young girl he was grilling was wasn't some sort of fair gendered serial killer, but that the true culprit, or culprits behind the missing assholes who deserved to go missing was one or more Bigfoot Sasquatch. Especially since his one fourth witch of a wife from the South Pacific had a bad habit of using her spells to control some of the weaker minded of this lot of creatures that are not supposed to even exist?

"Actually," Reynolds said, "she's not upset. That's what's getting me about the whole thing, and it's why I've come to you. It's as if this girl knows something."

"What else do you know about her?" Drake asked, his curiosity piqued. Could it be, he thought, that he might have a young, cryptozoologist in the making on his hands, here?

"Just that she came over here from Appalachiastan. First generation college student. No family to speak off. Her mother died when she was a teen."

"And you said her name was Jane?" Drake asked.

"Yeah," Reynolds said. "Jane (last name omitted from this text due to legal purposes)."

"You don't know what part of Appalachiastan she's from, do you?" Drake asked.

"I can't remember," Reynolds said. "She said it was somewhere down toward the southern part. Just above the coal fields. Timber country."

Drake looked off to one side, as if in deep thought. "Could it be?" he said, barely audible.

"Could it be what?" Reynolds asked.

"Give me a few minutes to shower up and I'll meet you at the station. I need to see this girl."

"What's going on here?" Reynolds asked.

"Maybe nothing," Drake said. He paused for a moment, and then he said, "maybe a lot."

****

Dick's actual name was Richard, but everyone called him Dick. He always knew that was because Dick was short for Richard, but he also knew that most people that knew him, most, as in all, thought he was a dick. And he was a dick, and it was intentional, so he never took offense to any of it.

Dick, now in his late forties, had always been one of those guys that always did the right thing, as long as there was no harm toward himself to come from it. And he'd always been one of those guys that made sure to point out the wrong in others. He'd formed the habit, in childhood, of being a snitch- a tattle tale.

He'd learned something about himself early in life- something most people would find alarming if they weren't sociopathic themselves- and that was that he took great pleasure in watching others suffer or endure hardship. It got him off much like watching girl on girl porn did others.

Mind you, Dick was not violent. He did not physically abuse others, or even small animals, but he'd found, as a very young boy, that he gained a morbid sense of both stimulation and gratification out of watching others suffer.

He'd come across this discovery in a very odd way. When he was ten years old, his mother's brother, Dick's Uncle Rick, had come to stay with them. The man was sick, and he would eventually die in the family's guest room. Looking back on it, Dick might tell you he never concerned himself with what ailed Uncle Rick, and he hadn't, but he fully understood now, as an adult, that his Uncle Rick had been one of the first wave of Americans who was not gay, a drug addict, or a poor black man to die from AIDS. Uncle Rick had been an unsafe manwhore. Professionally, he'd been a cop, and he was always screwing around on his wife, and it wasn't a secret at all. When he'd contracted the virus, and needed homecare, as he lay dying, slowly, his wife, fortunate not to have been infected by her adultrous manwhore husband, threw him out on his ass. Rick went to his little sister's house (Dick's mother), and there, in the words of William Faulkner, he lay dying, until he died. And until he did, his service revolver and badge lay on the nightstand beside him.

While Uncle Rick lay dying, Dick spent much time with him, listening to story after story from copland. Dick was enthralled by just how stupid some of the criminals Uncle Rick had busted had been. And as Uncle Rick's mind began to go more and more, he'd even shared the occasional story of some of his more adultish exploits.

These adult stories didn't do much for Dick, but once, when his younger brother was told to clean up Uncle Rick's bed mess (Uncle Rick was always making a mess, and the boys were to take turns, along with their mother, cleaning them up), and had got caught up in lying, claiming he'd already had his turn, when his mother knew he clearly had not, and he had gotten punished, corporally, for the first time ever (Dick's mother has reached her wit's end), and right in front of Dick, Dick felt his nether regions swell with blood. It was the first time in his young life this had ever happened, except for on times when he'd awakened with a full bladder, and though he could not explain the experience, he discovered that he very much liked it.

Shortly after this experience, while at school, he witnessed one of his classmates cheating on a test. The student, another boy, continually leaned over to view the answers on a girl's answer sheet at the desk beside him. Simply the thought of this other student being punished for his dirty deed was enough for Dick to experience the rapid blood flow to a certain appendage of his body. Without realizing he was walking across the classroom with what he and his friends would be referring to as a "pitched tent" just a few years later, Dick strode to the teacher's desk and ratted out the cheating student. Being that these were the days before "no such thing as a wrong answer" in the public schools, and the days when bad behavior was not given a diagnosis and a prescription, the offending student was summarily pulled into the hallway and given three swift smacks across the ass with a two inch thick board, known the the old days, as a paddle. With the sound of the third smack, Dick felt something that was not urine oozing into his underwear.

And thus, a quesa sadist was born.

Later, after school, the boy who'd gotten the paddling due to Dick having narked him out caught up to Dick on the way home and taught Dick, first hand, the saying, "snitches get stitches, bitches!" Dick found himself experiencing pleasure from this experience as well.

And thus, a masochist was born!

Sadist plus masochist equals sado-masochist.

So thus, a sado-masochist was born!

Dick, however, was a shy boy, and he found himself very much enjoying voyeurism as well. Not in any traditional sense, such as peeping on the girl or the boy next door as they undressed to shower or change. More like a "Needful Things" kind of way. Yes, a nod to the Stephen King work, here, where the old man would pit people off against each other and take pleasure in their infighting.

Dick learned early how to spot people who didn't like each other. He learned how to pit them off against each other. He learned how to hide in the bushes, behind the edge of a building, or between vehicles, and take pleasure in pleasuring himself as the two enemies squared off. He learned that the suffering didn't have to be physical. He learned to have his fellow students sent to detention, where he'd often climb a tree outside of the school and peer into the windows of the detention room and pleasure himself while the slew of students, many of whom were there because of his tattle tale ways, spent two agonizing hours after school, sitting at their empty desks, doing nothing.

After high school, Dick didn't waste any time heading off to college. He knew exactly what he wanted to do. He wanted to be a police officer just like dear dead Uncle Rick. He went to the academy and started out as a local sheriff's deputy after graduation. During his short stint as a sheriff's deputy, he went after old grudges. The guys who maybe got the attention from the girls he'd always crushed on but didn't have the balls to talk to himself. One of his favorites was following around the people who he knew were stoners and busting them for smoking a joint. He would often go as far as to throw them in the back seat of his cruiser, under the cover of darkness of night, and sit in the front and masturbate, unbeknownst to them, as they pleaded with him not to file charges for their simple, recreational use of God's magical green leaves. Their exclamations of suffering from glaucoma always brought him to climax. Usually, though he hated the bastards, he'd let them off, only so he could follow them around and bust them again later.

Dick's career skyrocketed when the opioid crisis hit the rust belt. An Ohio native and resident, his small town was hit extremely hard. It didn't help that the region bordered Appalachiastan, which was totally devastated during the crisis.

Dick took part in a large sweep that ended up netting sixty eight potheads and pill poppers one morning, and as he watched dozens upon dozens of druggies thrown into the police vans, all pleading for leniency, Dick found himself having to actually leave the scene due to his levels of hyper excitement. The part of it all that made it so exciting was not so much the sheer numbers of people suffering, but the fact that he'd helped set the sting up. He'd actually given a large portion of the drugs being confiscated to the dealers, in order for them to sell them to the users, making sure the bust would be like shooting fish out of a barrel.

"That's it!" he said to himself while changing underwear, though he knew his efforts were more than likely futile, as he'd no doubt be needing to change again in only a short while. "I have foiled my own plot! I am ready to join the F.B.I.!

And he did!

It took him a while to climb the ranks, but Dick eventually made his way into a lead detective role with the F.B.I., and this was where he'd spent the ten years prior to coming to county sheriff deputy Burt Reynolds' jurisdiction setting up and busting minor marijuana infracters for major crimes. Nothing made a dime bag dealer squeal like making sure to set him up with pounds and pounds of weed one day, and then coming by the next day and starting the ball rolling to have them sent up for the next twenty years. The climax after climax that came with each foiled plot was indescribable.

But then the states started legalizing the shit, and it had almost driven Dick to sheer impetence.

But then there were all the unsolved serial killer cases. Oh, how Dick did love a knowingly innocent person squirming in the back of his unmarked suburban after having been picked up for questioning in regard to a cold case involving someone the accused, momentarily by him, at least, had never even heard of. And since the windows on his unmarked suburban were blacked out, dark as night, he could pleasure himself up front, in the middle of broad daylight, while the accused cried like a baby and begged in the backseat after having been told that they would never see the sun or the moon again for the rest of their lives.

In a word, Dick was one twisted, demented fuck of a human being. He would have been an excellent counter sick fuck for an entire season of the old serial killer show 'Dexter.' But since he was part of the long arm of the law? It was society who would pay for his twisted ways, not him.

And now, Jane sat across the table from him in the questioning room in sheriff deputy Burt Reynolds' offices, as Reynolds, along with Dr. (honorary) Drake watched from the other side of the two way mirror.

***

"Is he jerking off?" Drake asked.

"He's trying," Reynolds said. The two men watched as Dick was clearly rubbing his dick, though his pants, underneath the table that separated him from the young college girl.

"She's really pretty," Drake said, "and I'm not judging, but Jesus, couldn't he wait until he got home?"

"I could tell you stories I've heard about this guy," Reynolds said, "that would make your skin crawl."

"So how do we handle this?" Drake said.

"I was hoping you'd have some ideas," Reynolds said. "I don't know what he expects to get out of this girl. But this is a dead end group of cases. You and I both know where it leads, and if we come out with the real culprit to all these unfortunate demises, they'll lock us up in the looney bin. How in holy hell are we supposed to save this girl from this creepy mother fucker without making ourselves look like a couple of lunatics?"

"I've got an idea," Dr. (honorary) Drake said, and he turned and headed toward the door to enter the questioning room. "Just go with it," he said, and then he turned the knob. Reynolds followed him into the questioning room.

***

"I helped her," Dr. (honorary) Drake blurted out as he and Reynolds burst into the questioning room. Jane looked up, her face still expressionless, and Dick quickly removed his hand from his dick.

"And just who the holy hell are you?" Dick asked.

"He's with me," Reynolds said. "I've had this guy in mind for this for a long time, and he's finally come clean." Drake thought Reynolds was doing an excellent job of following his lead so far, but, he also thought, with a name like Burt Reynolds, how could he not be a great actor?

"I'll take you to the remaining bodies you've not yet found out about," Drake said, "but you've got to promise leniency for the girl. I've been the mastermind the whole time, and I completely took advantage of her youth and inexperience."

"Are you willing to beg for her leniency?" Dick asked. Drake dropped to one knee and put his hands together, intertwining his fingers and resting them double clenched under his jaw. "Please," he said. "I am begging you now."

Dick almost creamed his khakis.

***

Dick pulled his unmarked suburban to the wide spot in the road where Dr. (honorable) Drake had instructed. They were in the middle of nowhere now, with Reynolds riding shotgun and Drake and Jane in the back.

Dick had allowed Drake his one phone call, by way of his cellphone, while driving to their destination. Drake had called his beautiful Pacific island princess of a wife, and said something about, "remember that time at the rocky overlook on our favorite trail? Out where the wild blueberry bushes cover the mountainside? It would be great for one last trip there, if only to smell the wonderful burning of a very powerful coconut husk." Dick had thought maybe it was some sort of code when he'd overheard it, but how on earth could such a ridiculous statement be code?

"Why are you doing this?" Jane had asked Drake after he'd hung up the phone. "This is the craziest bullshit I've ever been put through, and I'm going to make this dick internet famous the minute this is over. I know a couple of Asian chicks," she'd caught herself and she had amended her statement, "well, they're not really Asian," she'd said. "They're from Georgia. But I think they're Korean, ethnically, but my point is, they have a really successful YouTube channel, or Instagram or TikTok, or something, and I'm going to ruin this guy's career the minute this bullshit is done with."

"You're not gonna have that opportunity, sweet cheeks," Dick had said from the front seat. "Everybody out. You fucking soon to be folons lead the way. No funny shit."

The group started walking through the woods, Dr. (honorary) Drake leading the way. Jane was a couple of paces behind him, then Reynolds, and Dick was pulling up the rear, his right hand holding his service revolver, and his left resting just over his crotch.

"I think you'll find," Drake said to Jane, giving her a solemn look back over his shoulder as he did, "that it would be best to say nothing about any of this when it's all over." Jane gave him a look that let him know understanding was beginning to enter her mind and then he faced forward again, making sure to watch where he was going so he would not trip. "By the way," Drake said. "You remind me of someone I used to know. A long, long time ago."

"I bet you say that to all the girls young enough to be your daughter," Jane said.

"Seriously," Drake said. "Reynolds mentioned you were from Appalachiastan. What part?"

"It's all one part," she said, stepping over a fallen branch.

"Yup," Drake said. "True hillbilly."

"Fuck you, yuppie!" Jane said.

"I might look like a yuppie," Drake said, laughing lightly as he did. "But I can guaran-Goddamn-tee you I'm more hillbilly than you are."

"Yeah, right."

"Girl, I was spot lighting deer and skinning them and butchering them up before the sun came up in the middle of summer time years before you were born. I've dug ramps in two feet of snow, caught trout in subfreezing temperatures, and suffered heartache after heartache every time the Mountaineers had a winning season only to get slaughtered in whatever bowl game they went to."

"Really," Jane said, her voice softer.

"Really," Drake said. "I am a tried and true Cavalier fan for life now. I've adopted this place as my home town, but it ain't where my roots sprouted."

"That's enough," Dick said from the back. The group had walked nearly half a mile into the woods. "Where the hell are we going, anyway?" he asked.

"Right over there," Drake said, pointing to an outcropping of rocks where a steep incline began.

"Oh, my God," Jane said, not seeing what waited, hidden, behind the rocks, but feeling its presence with every bit of her empathic abilities. She looked at Drake and said, "You mean you can..." and she trailed off.

"You're not the only one," he told her. "There aren't many of us, but there's a few of us."

"How long have you been able to..."

"Shut, the fuck up!"

It was Dick. He was clueless as to the significance of the conversation he was interrupting, but he wouldn't have believed the idea of the subject matter anyway.

"This has gone on long enough. Everybody stop, and nobody move!" Dick walked up to Drake and got right in his face. "Show me!" he demanded.

"See that log sticking out over the last big boulder on the right?" he asked.

"Yeah," Dick said, looking over where Drake was suggesting.

"Just go to that log. Look around the other side of that boulder and you'll see the bodies. At least what's left."

Dick was so excited. He didn't even attempt to hide the erection which was rising in his pants. He would be able to threaten to have the girl executed, causing this Drake guy, who seemed so stoic, to beg for her life so much the memories of it alone would later allow Dick to fill the spank tank in his mind. He would probably be able to retire.

"What's your folks' names?" Drake asked Jane as Dick made his way over to the rock outcropping. Jane confessed that she had no clue who her real daddy was. She told him her mother had never been sure. She told him her mother's name, and Drake said, "oh, shit."

"What?" Jane said, looking over at him quickly.

"I mean," he said, and then clasped his hands before his mouth and shouted, "a little more to your left," to Dick.

Jane didn't turn her glare away from Drake. Suddenly, she felt as if he were familiar to her as well. "Did you know my momma?" she asked. She had visions in her mind of a man, a man that looked like Drake, but younger, visiting her and her mother when she had been a little girl. They hadn't stayed long. Just long enough to say hi. The man had said something about taking the woman that was with him to meet someone. The only other thing Jane could remember about the events was that when the man came back out of the woods, a couple of hours later, the woman was not with him.

"Holy fuck!" Dick screamed from just to the side of the large boulder. Jane and Drake looked over at him. He was staring upward. Reynolds began making his way to Jane and Drake to see what they were witnessing, but he wasn't quick enough. What he was not in time to see, but what Jane and Drake clearly did see, was a huge, hair covered hand reaching quickly from behind the boulder. The hair covered hand grabbed Dick around the neck and both squeezed and lifted at the same time.

Reynolds reached Jane and Drake just in time to hear both a crunching sound and a light groan. All he saw were Dick's feet being sucked, it seemed, behind the boulder at a height of about four feet above the ground. "What the..." he said, and Drake said, "You don't want to know, though I know you already do."

"What now?" Reynolds asked.

"Well," Drake said. "We've got about a half mile's hike to figure it out."

***

By the time the group of three got back to the road, they had their story straight. Reynolds would radio one of his young deputies to come pick them up. They would tell the naive lawman that Dick wanted to investigate the area alone, and that he sent them all back and told them to arrange their own ride. Everyone already knew that Dick was a dick, so that part of the story would never be questioned.

Later, when someone would eventually find what was left of Dick's body? Well, that would all simply be written off to yet another bear attack. The group wasn't worried.

Jane pressed Drake on his knowledge not just of the Bigfoot Sasquatch that had been so readily available when and where they needed it, him or her to be (no *they*, as it had been alone), as well as what he might have known about her mother or her part of Appalachian. She couldn't shake the feeling she had that he somehow seemed familiar to her, and she kept thinking back to the memory from when she'd been so young.

"There's a lot I need to explain to you," is all he said the whole way back to the station. Once they got to the station, Reynolds got his squad car and offered the two rides home. They accepted.

When the squad car pulled up to Drake's house, he looked into the backseat at Jane. He'd been riding shotgun. "If you'd like to come in for a bit, I can explain a lot." Jane stared at him, a questioning look on her face, but she said nothing. "My wife is home," he said. "I have no inappropriate intentions. And I will be more than happy to drive you back to your dorm later. I bet you could use something to eat, anyway. Especially something other than cafeteria food. Have you ever had adobo?"

There was one thing Jane knew, and that was the intentions of men. She could tell that Drake was sincere, and she in no way deemed him to be any sort of threat.

"I can stay for a bit," she said.

Drake got out of the car and then walked around to the back of the driver's side of the car and opened the door for Jane. They both thanked Reynolds for the ride, and he told them not to worry about anything going forward, at least as far as Dick went, because he'd make sure to clear everything up.

"So he knows?" Jane asked as they watched Reynolds pull away in his cruiser. "I mean, about..."

"Yeah," Drake said. "He knows." He began walking toward the front porch of his house. Jane walked beside him. "He thought it was me, at first," he said. "But someone actually tried to kill me a while back, and he came around to the truth of it all."

"Who tried to kill you?" Jane asked.

"Some fucking inbred redneck who was obsessed with Bigfoot Sasquatch and thought I was making fun of dumbfucks like him who believe in it."

"But you don't do that," Jane said as they began climbing the stairs to the porch. "I mean," she said, trailing off. "You actually know the truth about these things. Like me. Why would someone think you were making fun of them for believing in them?"

"Because, my new young companion," Drake said, "people are fucking nutcases. And they are going to believe what they want to believe, and you cannot confuse them with facts once their minds are already made up."

Jane needed no further explanation. She was attending university in town, and she knew all too well what Drake was saying. She'd never run into so many educated fools in her life as there were on campus. Sure, many of them truly were intelligent, but as far as actual real world smarts went? Well, she was thankful for all she'd learned during her hard way of life coming up in Appalachiastan.

Drake opened the door and held it for Jane. "After you," he said. She walked in and he followed, closing the door behind himself. The two of them were greeted by a beautiful young Asian woman who didn't appear to be much older than Jane. Jane felt that the woman looked familiar somehow. Like she'd seen her around town. The post office, maybe?

"Who this?" the beautiful young Asian woman said.

"Jane," Drake said. "Meet my wife. The beautiful Mrs. Drake."

"Hello," Jane said.

"Honey?" Drake said. "Meet Jane...

...My daughter."

The End

(For now)

Through The Eyes Of Bigfoot Sasquatch

Dark.

Lighter.

Gray. Mist.

Chirp, chirp, chirp.

Peep, peep.

Stretching. Yawning.

Sitting.

Standing.

Moving forward.

Inside new place. Wooden walls. Piles of hay.

Flashback:

"I swear to Jesus Christ as my witness, if that's that goddamn fox that got 'ol Perty, I'mma fill its face with lead!"

The other one said, "do you kiss your momma with that mouth?"

"Yes. And I go to church twice every Sunday and never miss a Wednesday evening worship. That's how goddamn tired I am of this son of a bitch gettin' my chickens!"

The other one said, "you can't kill foxes in this county. All them rich folks up at the hunt club made sure of it with the commissioner. Or the board. Or whoever the hell makes the laws at the county level. You better not shoot no fox, or your ass is goin' to jail."

Ducking into new place. Large wooden building. Hay. Hide in hay. Don't move!

"Ain't nobody goin' to jail for killin' no chicken killin' fox!"

The other one said, "you know how it is around here. Fuckin' animals have more rights than humans. I blame the goddamn university crowd."

"Awe, it looks like that son of a bitch got away again!"

The other one said, "come on now. Let's get back on in the house. It's freezing out here, and our beer's gettin' cold!"

"Fuck you! You chicken thieving son of a whore!" (Loud. So loud ears hurt.)

Watching them leave through crack in side of wooden walls. See them enter house. Light outside goes off.

Rip open feathery dead thing.

Eat warm insides.

Sleep...

Morning-

Walking past house. Looking in window. Two men sleeping. One on couch. One on floor.

Walking away from house. Into woods.

Trees. Bushes.

Hills.

Creek.

Drink.

Water cold.

Walking more.

Hungry.

Find food place.

Walking more.

Close. Closer. Closest.

Here.

Vroom, vrooms. Vroom, vrooms.

Locked.

Locked.

Open.

Bag. Large M.

Food!

Take.

Eat.

"Look at that, mommy!"

Little girl.

Big girl says, "look at what, honey?"

Drop to ground. Roll over embankment in front of vroom vrooms. Lay still. Don't move. Hide in tall grasses.

"It was a bear, mommy."

"A bear," says big girl. "You have a very vivid imagination, young lady. There's no bear out here. But there could be. You never know what you might see hiking on these trails."

"The bear went over the hill, mommy."

"Oh," said the big girl. "I get it. Did you guys sing that song in pre-school yesterday? The bear went over the mountain, the bear went over the mountain, the bear went over the mountain, to see what he could see!"

"No mommy. That's a stupid song."

"Now Sigma, why would you say that? That's not a nice word. Remember, sticks and stones may break our bones, but words will completely ruin our lives."

"I'm sorry mommy. But the bear really did roll over the mountain."

"Where?" the big girl said.

"Over there," the little girl said.

Tall one walks to edge of hill. Looks over.

Take deep breath and hold. Holding breath. Hold, hold, holding. Holding means cloaking. Can hold and cloak for long time. Giant lungs. Healthy lungs. Can hold breath and cloak for long, long time.

"There's nothing there, honey."

"Why are the weeds smooshed down right there?"

"Maybe a deer slept there last night."

"It would have been a big deer."

Hold breath longer. No problem. Can hold breath long, long time. Hold breath. Can't see me. Hold breath. Can't see me.

"Come on, honey. Let's go. Daddy's coming home for lunch today."

"Why is my car door open, Mommy?"

"Son of a bitch!" the big girl says. "Goddamn degenerates!"

"Words, Mommy," the little girl says. "Your words. You're going to destroy someone's life with your words."

Doors shut.

Vroom vroom starts. Leaves. Can hear it rolling away.

Breathe again. Can be seen again.

Sit.

Eat contents of bag with M on it.

Gross.

Greasy.

Hurts heart.

Spit rest out.

Rise.

Walk.

***

Later that afternoon…

***

Napping in bushes beside old country store.

Sun high. Energy low.

Must sleep.

Can't sleep.

Voices. Coming from bench in front of store. Too loud.

"Did you hear the one about the 'ol boy was sitting out here last week? Looked over and saw 'ol Clem's dog just a lickin' his nuts?"

"No," the other one said.

"'Ol boy said he wished he could do that, too. Why, I told him he could go on over there and try it, but that old dog would probably bite his face off."

"That one's older than you are," the other one said.

"Well let's hear you tell one, goddamn it!"

"I ain't gotta tell a 'ol worn out joke," the other one said. "I can just tell you what happened to my nephew Mark last week."

"That queer nephew of you'rn considers hisself a actor?"

"That's the one," the other one said. "But he ain't a queer, and he ain't a actor. He got him a girl prettier than you ever seen, and he's a entertainer. Magician."

"If he got a girl, he's a pretty good magician. Magic enough to make people think he ain't a queer."

"Well," the other one said. "Could be. You never really know with people. Especially family."

"So what happened to that queer nephew of your'n that's so worth telling?"

"Well," the other one said. "He was on his way over to Harrisonburg to do a show at JMU."

"That's where I'm tryin'a get my grandkids to go," the first one said. "Ain't as goddamn liberal as the university down in Charlottesville."

"Do you wanna hear it, or don't ya?" the other one said.

"Oh, go on and tell it, then."

"So he was headin' over there on thirty three west, and he got pulled over by the poe lease."

"What the poe lease pull him over for?"

"If'n you'll just shut the hell up, I'll tell ya."

"Oh, go on then," the first one said.

"Well, my nephew Mark said the poe lease pulled him over for speedin'. Asked him why he was goin' so fast, and well, Mark told him he was a magician of sorts, and that he had 'im a show over there at JMU.

"Well, that poe lease man told him that if he could juggle somethin' for him, he wouldn't write him a ticket. Mark told 'im he'd sent all of his equipment ahead with his lovely assistant.

Now, that would be that pretty girl I was tellin' you about. And he said he did't have anything to juggle.

"So the poe lease tells him he's got some flares in the back of his squad car. Mark tells him, alright, he'll juggle those.

"So the poe lease man lights five flares up and hands them to Mark. He's a jugglin' 'em all, real nice, right there beside the road. All of a sudden, some yuppie, probably from over here in Charlottesville, seein' how there's so many yuppies here and all, pulls over to the side of the road in his BMW. He gets out and goes over and lets himself into the backseat of that poe lease man's car.

"So the poe lease man walks over and asks the yuppie what he's'a doin' and the yuppie tells him to go on ahead and haul 'im in, because there ain't no way in holy hell he's gonna be able to pass that field sobriety test."

"Ah, ha, ha, ha! you old son of a bitch!" the first one said. "You done went and got me good! Hey, you know the difference between a BMW and a porcupine, don't you?"

"What's that," the other one asked.

"With a porcupine, the pricks are on the outside!"

Ah-ha-ha! Loud laughing from both.

Porcupine!

Ouch!

Sit half up! Fast. Turning. Looking for porcupine!

"What was that!" first one says. "Did you hear that?"

"Hear what?" the other one said.

"In the bushes. Behind us."

"Where in the bushes?"

"At our six, you dumbass! Where else would they be if I said behind us?"

Hold breath. Cloak. Hold breath. Can't be seen.

"Ah, it was probably just one of them old dumpster cats," the other one said. "Come on. It's well past noon. Let's get us a case of somethin' cheap and take it out to my place and get ta drinkin'. Faye's done gone over't'er sister's again. Prolly won't come back 'til tomorah."

***

Several hours later.

***

Walking along fence line. Sun heading lower.

BANG!

"Aurgh!" ears hurt.

Bang!

Bang!

"Aurgh!" ears hurt.

Changing direction. Walking over hill. Look down into open meadow through woods.

See man.

Crazy man. Slamming hammer down on steel anvil, driving anvil into wood.

Hat on inside out. White tag waving in breeze.

Man holding up red circle. Man talking into small thing in hand.

Walking closer.

Hiding behind trees.

Creeping.

Holding breath. Clocking. Can't be seen while holding breath. Creep to just inside tree line of field.

"What was that?" crazy man says, staring at small thing holding in hand. "Did you hear that?" Crazy man looks around. Eyes wide. Hat still on inside out. Why is hat on inside out? Man is crazy.

Crazy man holds up red circle again. "Right there," crazy man says. "It's like, I heard footsteps from something walking, but there's no one or nothing there. But I clearly heard footsteps. Rewind and listen."

Crazy man moving small thing in hand around. Pointing small thing in hand everywhere. "Get my six," crazy man with inside out hat says.

Have to breathe. Must breathe.

Deep breath. Ducking behind tree.

"Did you see that?" Crazy man says. "That tree back there. At my eight o'clock. I saw movement. Rewind and watch again."

Crazy man walks back toward middle of field. Crazy man talking to small thing in hand. Crazy man talking fast, then slow. Fast then slow.

Follow crazy man. Crazy man entertaining. Where crazy man flares? Crazy man juggle? Follow crazy man to find out.

"What's that!" crazy man says. Stops in field. "Okay, get my six. And as I was saying. Do I believe in Bigfoot Sasquatch? What about all the people who claim to have had sightings?

"Here's what I think about all those who've claimed to have seen Bigfoot Sasquatch," crazy man says. "I think half of them are lying, and I think the other half are not telling the truth."

This man crazy. Must follow crazy man.

Hold breath. Cloak. Walk. Stop.

"Did you hear that?" crazy man says. "It's like, there's something walking in this meadow with me. Something that can be heard, and felt with my spidey senses, but not seen. Rewind and see if you can see the sawgrass moving."

Crazy man very aware. Better hold breath long time. Crazy man not crazy.

"So here's what I mean by that. Okay, it is so obvious a great percentage of these assholes who claimed to have seen Bigfoot Sasquatch are simply lying. I don't know why. Maybe they want attention. Maybe they committed a crime and they want to blame it on their imaginary accomplice, Bigfoot Sasquatch. Maybe they are gaslighters who want to make others question their sanity. I don't know.

"But the other half? They are not telling the truth. However, I do not think they're lying. There's a difference. I do believe there are people out there who have seen things or had experiences that cannot be explained, and they attribute it to Bigfoot Sasquatch. Maybe, in their mind's eye, that's what they believed they saw when they got the glimpse of a bear, or a moose. Or they saw an actual human being from a far distance walking in the woods."

Gotta breathe.

Exhale.

Inhale.

Hold.

"Did you see that?" crazy man says. "It's like, there was something there, and then there wasn't. Rewind and watch. And with that said, I'm going to lay this drumstick here on the gifting stump and head in for the night. Thanks for joining me for another episode of the PBS...

"...S...

"The potential, Bigfoot... Sasquatch...

"...show."

Crazy man stop talking to small device in hand. Crazy guy push buttons on small device. Crazy guy walking toward house. Crazy guy going in house.

Breathe.

Dark now.

Tired.

Hungry.

Pick up drumstick crazy man left on stump.

Eat.

Put bone back so crazy man won't know.

Go inside crazy man's outbuilding.

Lay down on pile of hay.

Sleep.

The End

(At least for another day in the life of Bigfoot Sasquatch)

*Make sure to read all of the other Bigfoot Sasquatch Files volumes by Kevin E Lake, if you've not already, and make sure to check back for more, soon. All of Kevin E Lake's other works- full length novels and other short story collections- are available in print or Kindle from Amazon.

Made in the USA
Monee, IL
03 March 2021